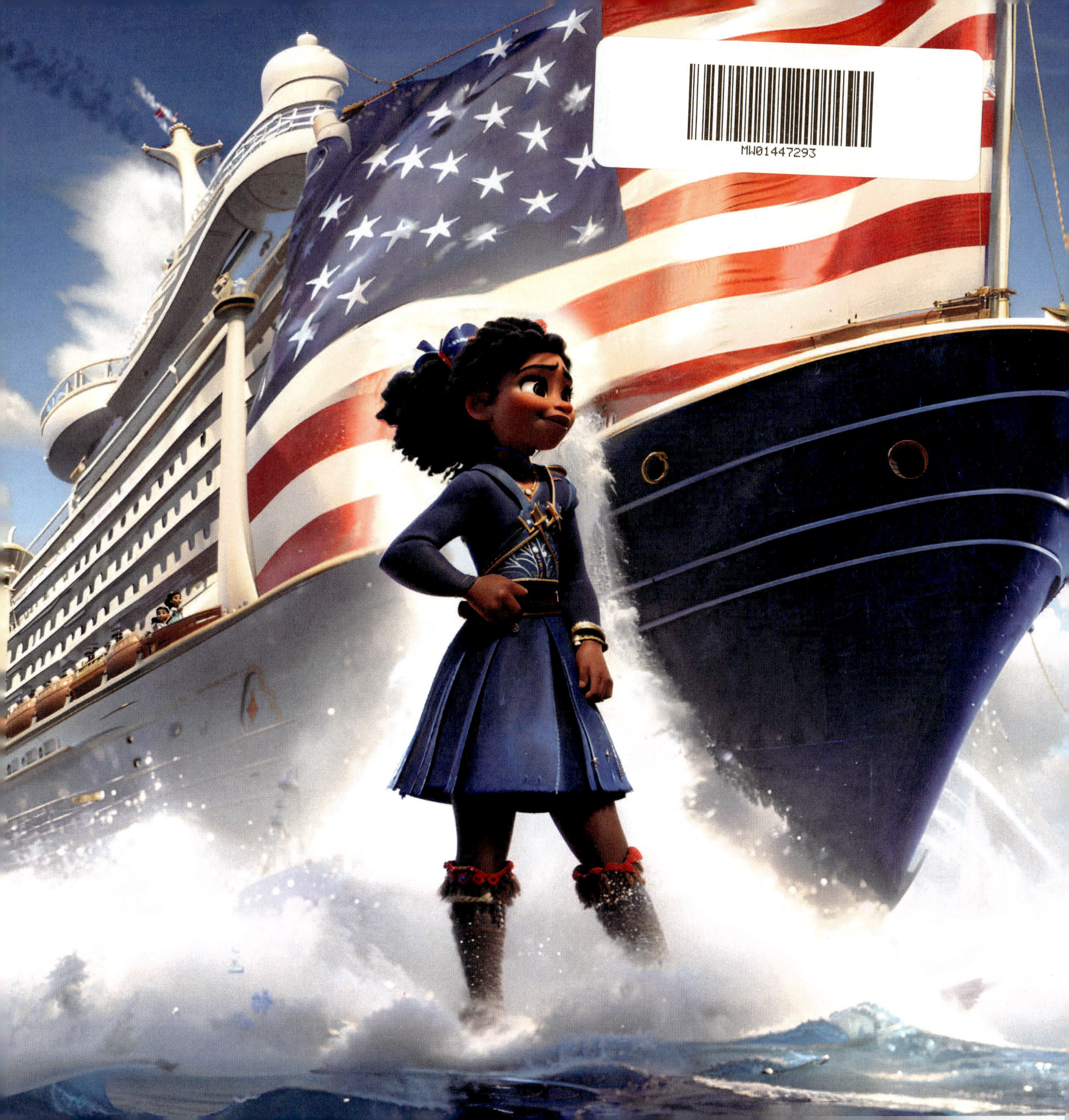

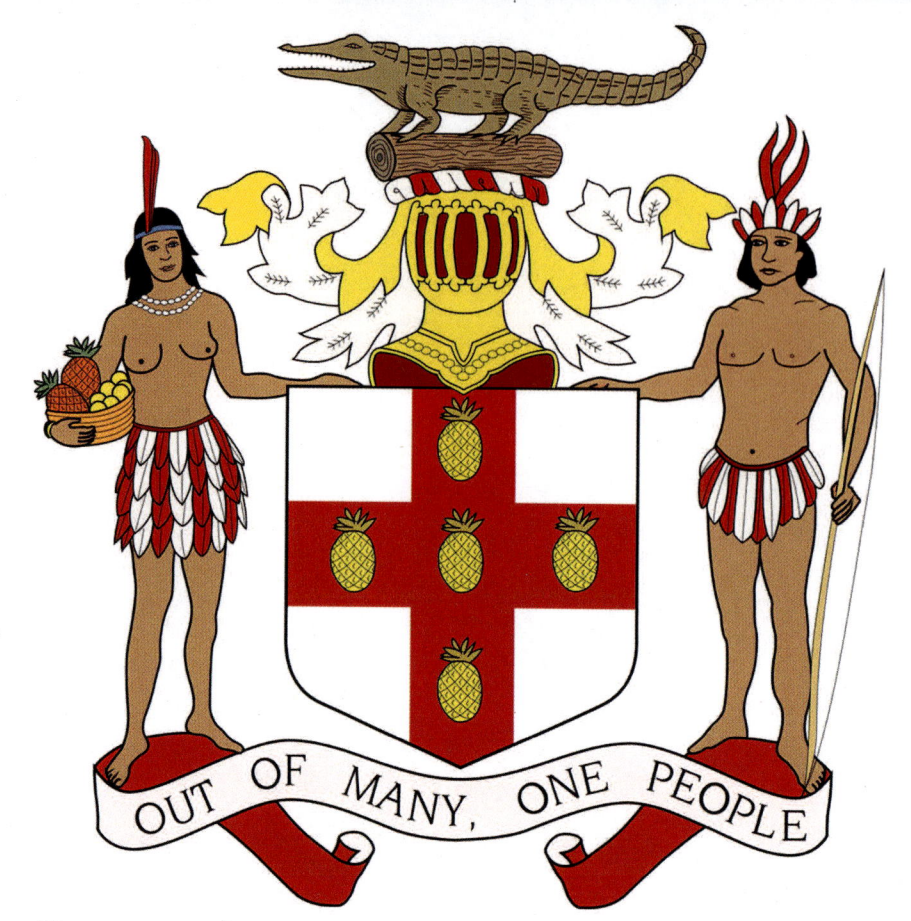

The Jamaican Coat of Arms contains the national motto.

Princess Zee Comes To America: An Immigration Tale About Perseverance In Faith
Text and Illustrations Copyright © 2023 by Tom B. Free

No part of this book may be used or reproduced in any manner whatsoever without written permission except in the case of brief quotations embodied in critical articles and reviews.

www.TomBFree.com

ISBN Kindle eBook 978-1-960735-07-2 Softcover 978-1-960735-08-9 eBook 978-1-960735-09-6
This artist used multiple digital tools to create the paintings and 3D rendered-like illustrations.
First Edition

This book is dedicated to the real Princess Z, my daughter,
a Jamaican princess in every sense of the word... at least to me.
This story is a real story but it's also an old story.
Many have made the journey to American shores and it's always
been hard. Modern immigration is difficult in new ways,
but the lesson we can learn is to keep on pushing forward
even when the way ahead is not easy.

As such, this book is also dedicated to American immigrants
of the past, present, and future. May God bless your efforts!

LADIES IN DISTRESS, and KNIGHTS OF VALIANT DEEDS.
Dragons SPEWING FIRE, Rearing Noble Steeds.
In caverns gleaming with HIDDEN CHESTS OF GOLD,
ADVENTURES begin as EPIC TALES unfold.

Of Royalty and Princesses, we oft hear,
In Lofty Castles with Prince Charming near.
Fairy Tales... though Wondrous and Grand,
Often stem from humble, unassuming land.

From Rags to Riches, the Stories we Know,
A Journey Ahead, a Path to Sow.
For even Princesses start SMALL,
Work their way UP, Rising Above it All.

As the curtain ascends, the LIGHTS SHINE with MIGHT,
Unveiling a world yearning for its Story to take Flight.

Once Upon a Time in a Faraway Land,
A girl named Zee, Many dreams she planned.
She lived within Jamaica's heart, a farming town serene,
No lavish castle, just fruit fields lush and green.

Princess Zee dreamed of a Different Place,
An *Adventure* ahead, a New Kind of **Race**.

Longing to be an American Princess in the **USA**,
To start a new life, succeed in a different way.

Leaving her home wouldn't be Easy,
Obstacles ahead, that was clear to See.
But Princess Zee was *Brave* and *Strong*,
She knew she could do it, it wouldn't take long.

Would it...?

Zee's family sparked the **FLAME**, igniting her desire,
To leave Jamaica and reach Higher and Higher.

With Auntie Dannie, Uncle Jam so near,
And Grandma Paula, Called Mommy dear.
Zee played with cousins, and brother Prince Jay,
Each day a JOY, in every way.

Her home a paradise on Earth, oh so fair,
But struggles Abound, a family's hardship to bear.
Her Mother moved away, across the sea,
To work in America, the LAND OF THE FREE.

No castle, no gowns, no crown, but Zee had a goal,
The girl aimed high, with all of her soul.
A girl who knew who she was from the Start,
A princess based on her **Royal Heart**.

ROYAL CHARACTER STATS
- FAITH
- LOYALTY
- PURITY
- INTEGRITY

Princess Zee, a ROYAL so true,
With a **HEART OF GOLD**, shining through.
Not based on where you're from, or skin so fair,
But on your Character, and how you **Care**.

No matter your origin, or the color of skin,
You can be a PRINCESS from within.
Moral virtue makes a royal shine,
Sons and daughters of the DIVINE.

A person's character makes them Royalty.
FAITH and purity is key, loyalty for all to see,
To truly live a life of integrity.

In hard times, a true heart's call,
Real royals rise, **SHINE ABOVE ALL**.
Sons and daughters of High King above.
In His care, we **Rise With Love**.

Facing tough times, a character is Tested.
In those moments, mere human strength is Bested.
Iron *sharpens* iron, so the proverb goes,
And through struggles, inner royalty shows.

Princess Zee's family, Too,
Faced struggles, trials Anew.
Jobs Hard to Find, life not grand,
Mother moved Away, to lend a hand.

Still... Mother visits each year,
The family beaming with **Love so Dear**.
Happiness abounds, in every way,
Together they laugh, in bright display.

With Mother working hard in the **UNITED STATES**,
Princess Zee longed for a chance to see her Face.
SURPRISE! A Shock Wedding, Mother married an American man!
Now Zee had a new Father, three brothers, a new family plan.

Prince Zaydon and Prince Ash,
New brothers for Zee In A Flash.
This new Father, his love he would express,
Lovingly calling Zee his little Jamaican Princess.

Excitement surged in Zee's heart, to meet her new **KING**,
Mother promised a future to `Take Wing`.
`FLY` to America, **LAND OF THE FREE**,
Hearts full of **GLEE**, they'd Immigrate as Family.

Though work was scarce, life in Jamaica felt fine,
The church stepped in, helped when there wasn't a Dime.
Family stayed united, through thick and through thin,
Supporting each other, with a Smile or a Grin.

Grandma Paula cooked meals, Hearty and Rich,
Rice and peas, tasty dishes made in a Pinch.
Princess Zee loved helping, especially with the yams,
And Grandma would listen to the girl sing sweet jams.

"Cover us Lord, with Your Blood," Zee would sing,
Invented by Mother, the tune made Spirits Take Wing.

Dreadlock-wearing Rastas, face of religion in the Nation,
Prim, Proper Protestant Church, the Main denomination.
Every Sunday people gathered, hearts full of His power,
Worshiping for many hours, under a humble tower.

Through the hymns, Zee found a way,
To connect with her Lord, and to pray.
Through her voice, her FAITH grew Strong,
For in church, found heart's truest song.

"In God We Trust", motto of the UNITED STATES,
Jamaicans know well, trust in God elevates.
For in the face of hardship, must take action and pray,
Trusting in the Almighty, to guide them every day.

Jamaica, though small, knows God's Immense Graces,
For Blessings come in, many a Shape and Spaces.
Little they have, yet in Him they put FAITH and TRUST,
Not just with their Lips, but in Actions Robust.

Jamaica the Beautiful, **Heart** of the Caribbean way,
An island nation, a tropical dreamland for play.
A blend of Ideas, a rich history,
A culture Unique, every corner a *mystery*.

The rolling hills, verdant countryside so green,
Jerk seasoning, OH What a Flavorful Scene.
Reggae music fills the air, a Joyful Sound,
Jamaica's natural beauty, Simply Profound.

Despite different cultures, unity is found,
A national motto, on which it's bound.
"Out of Many, One People" it rings,
Like America's, a similar thing.

"*E Pluribus Unum*", the words they say,
"Out of Many, One" in every way.

Despite loving Jamaica, Zee's eager heart was BRIGHT,
To fully leap and travel, cross ocean and unite,
With her hardworking Mother, in America's light.

Excited to see her new family, her new home set afar,
But immigration is a journey Long... hardly a shooting star.

The immigration process is slow, an emotional drain.
Weeks stretch into months and even years, causing much pain.

Not allowed a Christmas visit, not even a birthday.
The only recourse was for Zee, to have FAITH and PRAY.

Although Nothing replaced Mother, family filled **heart's hole**,
Bringing partial comfort and love, nourishing the young soul.

Aunty Dannie, "She's Simply the Best!",
Always there for, sharing in Zee's Quest.
Watching TV, sharing ice cream with glee.
Zee's sweet tooth, easy for all to see.
Weekly travel, a walk to the store,
Buying groceries, yummy snacks galore.

Once in a cab, to school did Zee depart.
When Dannie left, it saddened Zee's **heart**.

On the way home trees overhead, with fruits ripe and sweet,
Offered a treat for them to eat, while strolling down street.

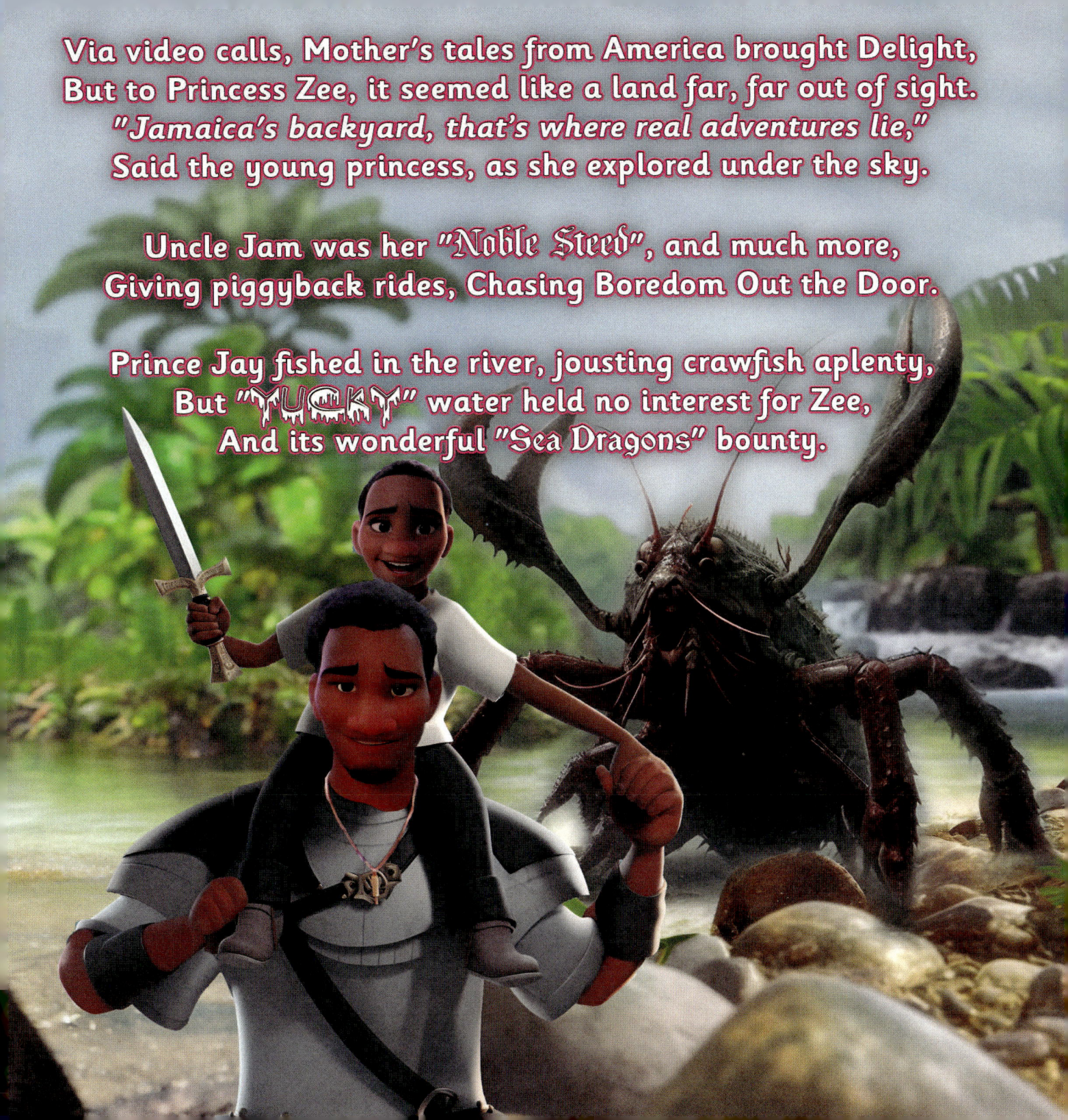

Via video calls, Mother's tales from America brought Delight,
But to Princess Zee, it seemed like a land far, far out of sight.
"Jamaica's backyard, that's where real adventures lie,"
Said the young princess, as she explored under the sky.

Uncle Jam was her "Noble Steed", and much more,
Giving piggyback rides, Chasing Boredom Out the Door.

Prince Jay fished in the river, jousting crawfish aplenty,
But "YUCKY" water held no interest for Zee,
And its wonderful "Sea Dragons" bounty.

When electrical surges doused the lights, Causing *FRIGHT*,
Phone flashlights came out to tell stories and LIGHT UP THE NIGHT.

Foolishness abounds, as they giggle and play,
Telling cheeky tales, to laugh the night away.

Zee's hero is Nanny of the Maroons, a legend with attitude,
Caught bullets with her hands and THREW them, Back at the dude!

At *First*, the stories are full of Laughter and Delight,
Then older brother turns the tale-spinning to Fright

There is one tale famous throughout the land,
A real-life Legend that everyone can understand.
The storytelling traveled afar, to a distant Parish land,
Comes the WHITE WITCH of Rose Hall, in a Great House so Grand.

Dead 200 years, some say the WHITE WITCH still walks the halls,
A GHOST glimpsed in photos, stalking *victims* with WAITING CLAWS.

That was **Real Life**, but this version adds a *Twist*,
In this tale, the GHOST, a lone princess will *resist*.

CREEPING AND CRAWLING through the hills east of Montego Bay,
The Princess ascended Rose Hall amidst moon's pale ray.

Princess confronted WHITE WITCH, Casting evil spirit DOWN,
But it was COURAGE and FAITH, that Prevailed, NOT her CROWN.

Faces beaming in the Light, the kids listened closely to the tale,
Wishing that they were all there, feeling **bold**, Inspired to Prevail.
So they finished their story, in the dead of night,
Filled with Dreamy Hope, and a sense of Delight.

For They Too could be Royals, with hearts Pure and Kind,
And never Give Up Faith... even when life was unkind.
Royalty is more than blood, wisdom these storytellers understood,
In facing adversity, true royalty is found in being Good.

They knew that true royalty comes from within,
With good character a faithful heart will Win.
Proving that true royalty resides within the soul,
Not just reserved for those swathed in gold and assigned the role.

With night stories complete, Princess Zee traveled away,
Visiting great grandparents, Momma and Papa, for a while to stay.
Together they ate, played games under the sun,
Enjoying the porch breeze, until the day was Done.

Like countless princesses, young Zee adored her dolls,
But her father's parents Lacked them, leaving her in pity's thralls.
Aunt Nor styled her hair, dressed Zee in regal guise.
With graceful stride, she roamed with *sparkling eyes*.
In realms of dreams and pure imagination,
Zee Reigns as PRINCESS of her own Creation.

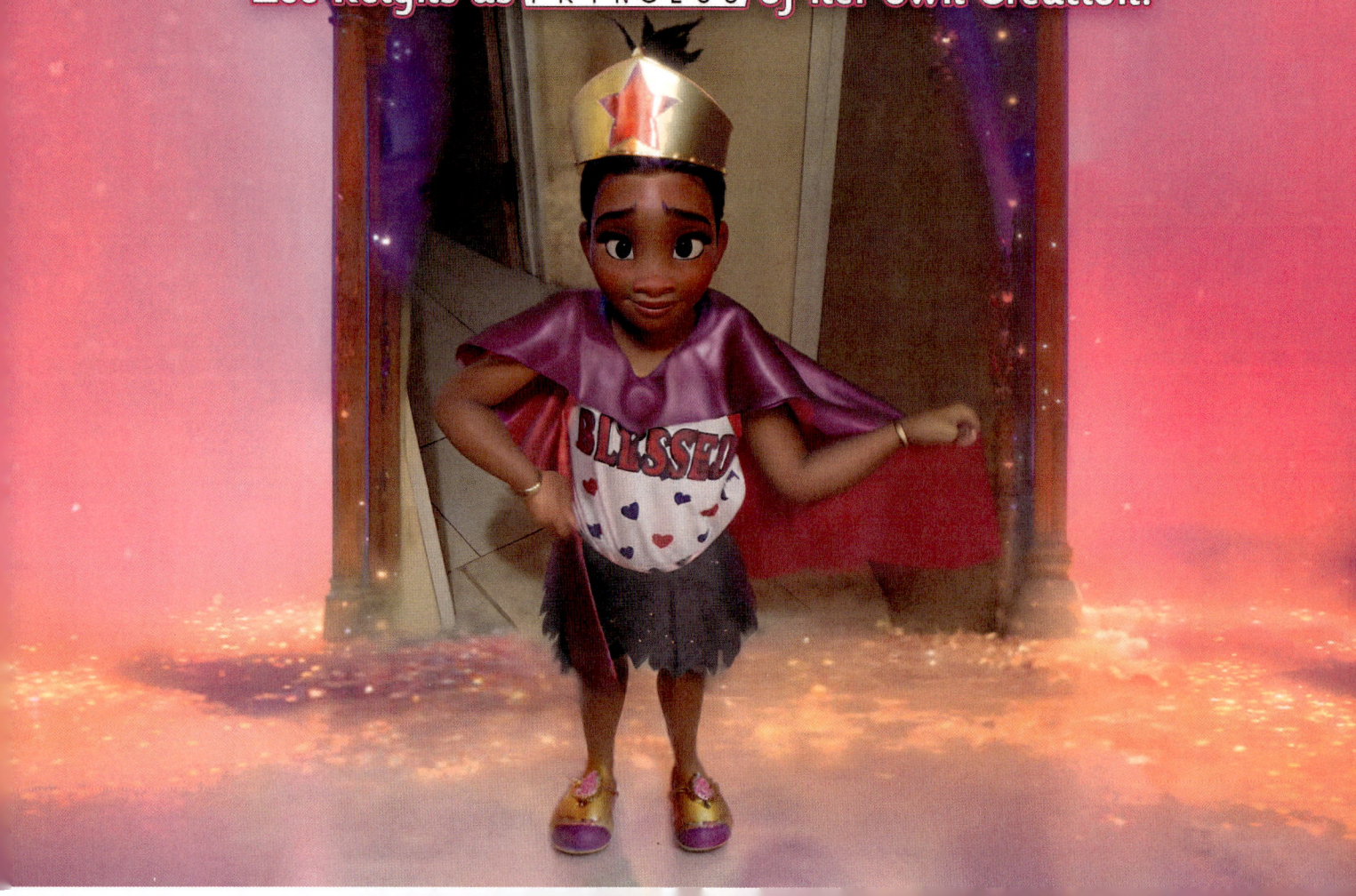

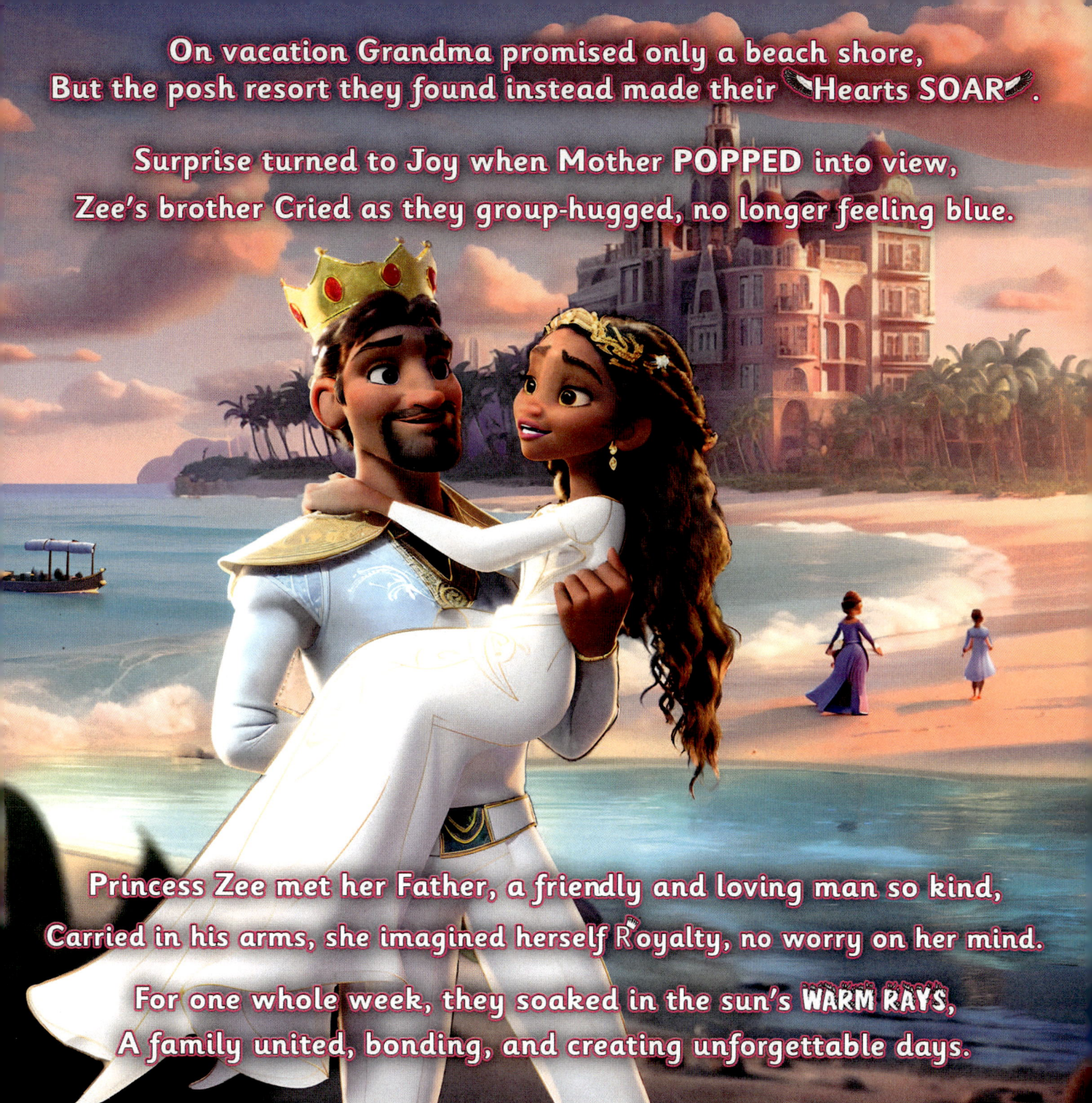

On vacation Grandma promised only a beach shore,
But the posh resort they found instead made their Hearts SOAR.

Surprise turned to Joy when Mother POPPED into view,
Zee's brother Cried as they group-hugged, no longer feeling blue.

Princess Zee met her Father, a friendly and loving man so kind,
Carried in his arms, she imagined herself Royalty, no worry on her mind.

For one whole week, they soaked in the sun's WARM RAYS,
A family united, bonding, and creating unforgettable days.

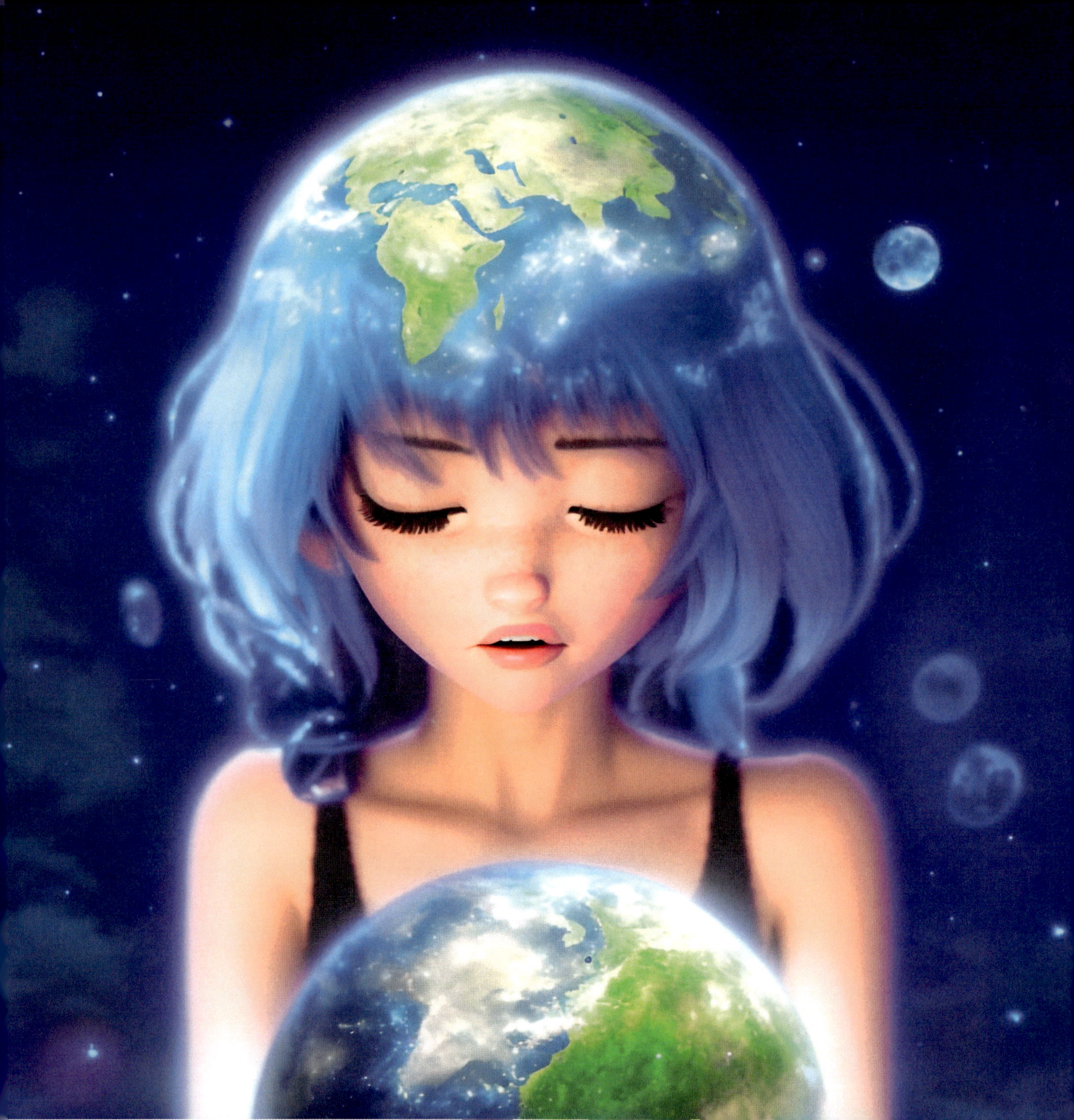

This brief respite of fun made it much easier to wait,
Suddenly the world was Different, a drastic Change of Fate.

A tragedy STRUCK, the sad children were told,
The pandemic *HIT*, lockdowns put life on hold.

Princess Zee and her brother Jay, no school anymore,
No visits with friends or relatives, all they had was Indoor.

Mother and Father couldn't travel, from Florida to See,
Their little Princess and Prince, it was a sad reality.

For Princess Zee, it was hard to wait another year,
To see her parents and new siblings, oh how she did fear,
That the day of departure would never draw near.

The family adapted, found new ways to connect,
VIRTUAL HUGS AND KISSES, video chats to Reflect.

But Princess Zee missed the warmth of a real embrace,
The feeling of her Father's arms, a familiar safe space.

She Missed *EXPLORING*, her brothers playing games,
And even their Fights... it wasn't quite the same.

Yet in her Heart, Hope burned with radiant light,
They'd reunite, her dream in faith made right.

For now, she had memories to cherish and keep,
Until the day they could all gather and Leap,
Into each other's arms and together they'd Weep.

Zee learned to Persevere, even as the SYSTEM wasn't Fair,
To pursue what was Right, without giving in to DESPAIR.

The PANDEMIC was hard, for families All Around,
But Zee knew that with patience, better times would be Found.

She trusted in the Lord's timing, HIS plans for her Life,
Found Peace in not being ANXIOUS, in this time of strife.

Every day she *prayed* for help, gave Thanks for what she had,
Knowing every good *gift* comes from above, and that made her glad.

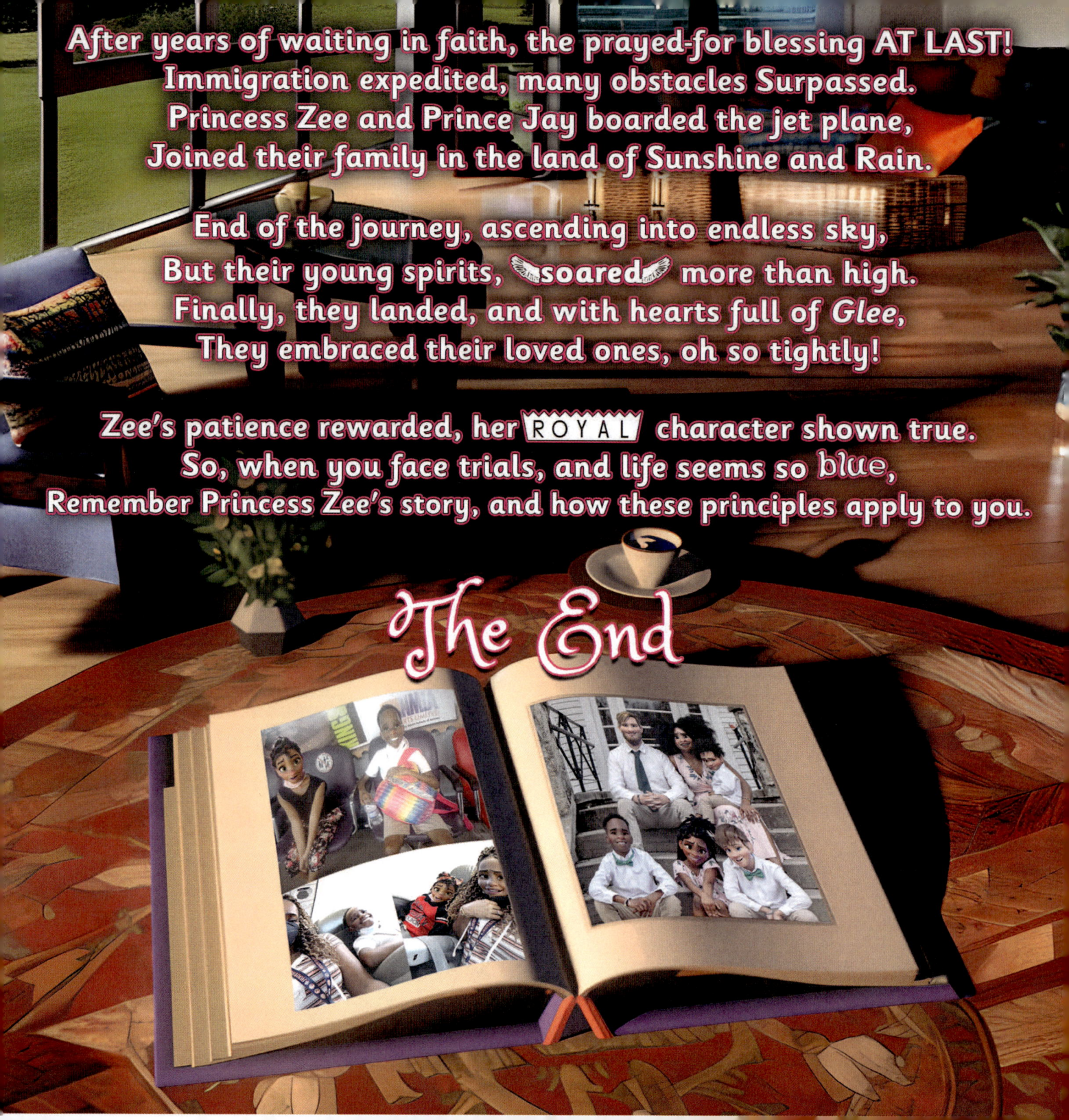

After years of waiting in faith, the prayed-for blessing AT LAST!
Immigration expedited, many obstacles Surpassed.
Princess Zee and Prince Jay boarded the jet plane,
Joined their family in the land of Sunshine and Rain.

End of the journey, ascending into endless sky,
But their young spirits, soared more than high.
Finally, they landed, and with hearts full of *Glee*,
They embraced their loved ones, oh so tightly!

Zee's patience rewarded, her ROYAL character shown true.
So, when you face trials, and life seems so blue,
Remember Princess Zee's story, and how these principles apply to you.

The End

Made in the USA
Columbia, SC
24 June 2023